Henry
AND THE GHOST TRAIN

by Christopher Awdry

illustrated by Ken Stott

A fair had come to the Island of Sodor. Men had set up stalls and rides near the junction. A notice on one of them said it was a GHOST TRAIN.

At the station everyone was talking about ghosts.
"What is a ghost train?" asked Henry.
"It is a tunnel that trains run through," his driver explained.

"It's full of ghosts and other spooky things."
"I'm not scared of stupid old ghosts," Henry said.
But he did not want to meet one, just in case...

That evening Henry's driver told him: "Part of the tunnel roof has collapsed. The Fat Controller says we must take some men to clear away the rubble."

"Bother," grumbled Henry. "I was looking forward to a rest." Still grumbling, Henry pushed two trucks and a van full of workmen into the tunnel.

He was going nicely when suddenly there was a
loud clanking noise.
"Your tender is off the line," said his driver.

"We must have run into some rubble. We can't go forward and we can't go back. We shall have to wait until the Fat Controller can sort something out."

It was very quiet in the tunnel. The workmen walked home and Henry dozed, but he woke up with a start. He was moving!

"Oooooooooooooh...er!" wailed a ghostly voice and
a white shape floated towards him. Henry was terrified.
His wheels were shaking but he hurried on.

Then he saw a station ahead. He felt much better now. He slowed down to stop, but when he saw what was on the platform he did not want to!

The station had a skeleton staff and a Very Thin Controller.
And waiting to catch the train was a vampire!

When he heard "poooop poooop" in the distance,
Henry felt better.
"That sounds like Gordon," he said.

But it was a ghostly, shadowy Gordon who rushed towards him with a scream and a roar.

Just as Henry felt he could bear no more,
he heard his driver's voice.

"Wake up, Henry," the driver said.
"Your tender is back on the line. We can go home now."

Henry was delighted. He went quickly back to the shed and had a long drink of water. He felt better after that.

But he was careful not to tell the other engines about the Ghost Train. He was sure they would laugh at him.

Percy
AND THE KITE

by Christopher Awdry
illustrated by Ken Stott

Lots of children were on their way to the grand kite-flying competition. "I want to fly a kite," said Percy dreamily.

"Engines don't fly kites," said Thomas. He remembered
what had happened when he went fishing.
Percy scuttled off to take some trucks to the woodyard.

The foreman checked in the delivery.
"I'd love to fly a kite," said Percy, still dreaming.

"My son, Jake, is flying a kite in the competition," said the foreman. "You watch for it – it's a special green one."

The weather that day was bright and sunny with a strong wind, just right for flying kites.

As Percy steamed to the harbour, the kites were racing into the sky. Soon he spotted a big green one.

"That green one is flying well," said Percy's Driver.
As they drew nearer, Percy thought he recognised it.
He was right – it was a green engine just like him.

"That must be Jake's kite," said his driver.
Percy was thrilled. "Peep, peep, it's me – I'm flying,"
he whistled happily.

On their return journey the wind dropped. The kites began to dip and dive towards the ground. One even fell into the lake.

"What will happen now?" asked Percy anxiously.
"When the wind blows again it will soon carry them up,"
said his driver.

At the next station they met Thomas.
"Feeling hungry, Percy?" he called.

Percy was puzzled. "What does he mean?" he asked.
"I haven't a clue," replied his driver.

Toby was waiting at the top station.
"When does the party start, Percy?" he asked.

Percy's driver jumped down from the cab. He looked at Percy's funnel and burst out laughing.

"Well, well, Percy," he exclaimed. "You've been flying a kite without knowing it." He unwound a string from Percy's funnel and showed him a kite like an iced cake.

Percy laughed. "So that's what you meant by a party, Toby," he said. "I wish we could really eat that cake."

They took the cake kite back to the field on their next journey. They arrived just in time to see the First Prize being given to ...

... Jake, for his kite shaped like Percy.
"I won, I won," whistled Percy excitedly. "That's even
better than flying a kite."

Well done, Percy and Jake.

Thomas

AND THE TIGER

by Christopher Awdry

illustrated by Ken Stott

Thomas and the engines were working very hard to help deliver
animals to the new wildlife park. Some animals came by lorry and
some by rail. The engines pulled extra trucks to carry them.

One morning Thomas's driver was very happy.
"We're going to the harbour today, Thomas," he said. "There is
something to collect for the wildlife park."

At the harbour there was a big crate with a tiger and her
cubs inside. The tiger had come from a zoo abroad.
A crane lifted the crate onto the truck and Thomas set off.

At the station Thomas waited while the big crate was
unloaded. He was quite sad to see the tiger go.

Thomas had been proud to carry such a beautiful animal.
"I wonder if I shall see it again," he thought.

Near the station was an old engine shed.
The men used it for storing things they did not use very often.

Later when Thomas was passing the shed he thought he saw something moving inside. It seemed to look stripy.

The next day Thomas was at the station. He was listening to his driver talking to the fireman.

"It says in the newspaper that a tiger has escaped from the wildlife park," said the driver. "I wonder where it is?" Thomas smiled. He knew.

"Look in the old engine shed as we pass," he told his driver.
When they came close, Thomas slowed down.

His driver looked out of the cab. "Why, it's the tiger and her cubs," he said. "That was very smart of you to find them, Thomas."

Thomas's driver told the Fat Controller about the tiger and her cubs at once.

"We'd better let her keeper know she's safe," said the
Fat Controller.

A lorry came from the wildlife park to collect the
tiger and her cubs. The keeper was very pleased.

"Well done, Thomas, for finding our tiger," he said, and the
Fat Controller agreed. "You've been a Really Useful Engine,"
he said.

Thomas often sees the tiger and her cubs when he passes the park now. He feels proud to have found her.